The Worst Day of My Life

A comedy

Alan Richardson

I0536634

New Theatre Publications - London

www.plays4theatre.com

The edition published in 2013

New Theatre Publications

2 Hereford Close | Warrington | Cheshire | WA1 4HR | 01925 485605

www.plays4theatre.com   email: info@plays4theatre.com

New Theatre Publications is the trading name of the publishing house that is owned by members of the Playwrights' Co-operative. This innovative project was launched on the 1st October 1997 by writers Paul Beard and Ian Hornby with the aim of encouraging the writing and promotion of the very best in New Theatre by Professional and Amateur writers for the Professional and Amateur Theatre at home and abroad.

ISBN 9 781 840 94920 9

Characters

Charlie Brown
Samantha
Joanne
Evelyn
Melissa

4

Copyright Information

Video-Recording of Amateur Productions

Performing Licence Applications

A performing licence for these plays will be issued by "New Theatre Publications" subject to the following conditions.

Conditions

1. That the performance fee is paid in full on the date of application for a licence.
2. That the name of the author(s) is/are clearly shown in any programme or publicity material.
3. That the author(s) is/are entitled to receive two complimentary tickets to see his/her/their work in performance if they so wish.
4. That a copy of the play is purchased from New Theatre Publications for each named speaking part and a minimum of three copies purchased for backstage use.
5. That a copy of any review be forwarded to New Theatre Publications.
6. That the New Theatre Publications logo is clearly shown on any publicity material. This is available on our website.

Fees

Details of script prices and fees payable for each performance or public reading can be obtained by telephone to (+44) 01925 485605 or to the address below.

Alternatively, latest prices can be obtained from our website www.plays4theatre.com where credit/debit cards can be used for payment.

To apply for a performing licence for any play please write to New Theatre Publications 2 Hereford Close, Warrington, Cheshire WA1 4HR or email info@plays4theatre.com with the following details:-

1. Name and address of theatre company.
2. Details of venue including seating capacity.
3. Dates of proposed performance or public reading.
4. Contact telephone number for Author's complimentary tickets.

Or apply directly via our website at www.plays4theatre.com

The Worst Day of My Life
a One Act Comedy by Alan Richardson
cast (in order of appearance)

Charlie Brown. . . . . *a hospital patient, late forties or older*
Samantha. . . . . *a young nurse*
Joanne. . . . . . *a hospital visitor, slightly younger than Charlie*
Evelyn. . . . . *another visitor, aged to match Charlie*
Melissa. . . . . *another visitor, also aged to match Charlie*

*(The age of the cast is open to flexibility. **Charlie**, **Evelyn** and **Melissa** can be anywhere from late forties to sixties or beyond, provided they are all roughly in the same age bracket. **Joanne** can be younger, but is still "mature" compared with **Samantha** - who should be as young as possible.)*

Time. . . . . *the present*

Setting   *A well appointed room in a large town or city hospital with one open entrance. There is a standard hospital bed with a bedside cabinet and a comfortable chair at one side. On the other side is a simpler chair. The only other items of furniture are a metal bin beside the cabinet and small functional table for meals with another two chairs beside it. Other items of hospital paraphernalia like a folding screen can be added to suit. On top of the cabinet is a very stylish get well card, a bottle of cherry cordial and a box of tissues in tasteful pastel colours. The appearance and placement of those and other props is vitally important. Suggested opening music- "As Time Goes By" from the film "Casablanca".*

*The curtains open on **Charlie** sitting on his bed reading a rather dog-eared paperback. A rather ordinary and unassuming man aged late forties or older. The dressing gown and pyjamas he is wearing are equally dull and plain. He glances towards the doorway, checks his watch, and then resumes reading. Moments later, **Samantha** Howard appears at the doorway. She is a vivacious and amiable young nurse. She wasn't exactly top of the class at Nursing College, but her heart's in the right place. The age gap between **Samantha** and **Charlie** should be as wide as possible.*

Sam   Good afternoon, Mister Brown.

Charlie   Afternoon, Nurse Howard.

Sam   *(looking over her shoulder before coming in)* Afternoon, Charlie.

Charlie	Say it again, Sam.
Sam	Good afternoon to you, Charlie. Sorry about the formal bit. But I got a row from sister yesterday for being "too familiar" with the patients. *(She begins a quick tidy of the room.)*
Charlie	Don't knock formality, Sam. It's all about respect.
Sam	I know. But it's like this hospital has put the clock back. Surnames only. Set visiting hours.
Charlie	Set times suit me fine. I like to be organised and plan ahead. Then I can cope with the unexpected… like this morning.
Sam	What happened? Don't tell me, no visitor?
Charlie	Afraid not. Which reminds me…
	(He looks at his dressing gown as if to reassure himself that he's wearing the right thing. He then removes the get well card from the top of his cabinet and replaces it with another from inside the cabinet. The replacement card is very plain. Next, he swaps boxes of tissues. The replacement is a supermarket name economy white box. Finally, the bottle of cherry cordial is switched for a simple bottle of mineral water.)
Sam	Well, that is a first for you. You've had a visitor three times a day since you arrived here.
Charlie	Not to worry. It gave me the chance to catch up my reading.
Sam	Now that book looks like it's been read a hundred and one times.
Charlie	Just about. It's my favourite. A bio on the life of Bogie.
Sam	Bogie?
Charlie	Humphrey Bogart.
Sam	Now I've heard of him. What team does he play for?
Charlie	No, Sam. Humphrey Bogart was an actor. The best.
Sam	Oh… I know who you mean. He was the young doctor in those old black and white comedy films. And "Death in Venice". He was good in that one.
Charlie	Wrong actor, Sam. You're thinking of Dirk Bogarde. Humphrey Bogart was Sam Spade in "The Maltese Falcon" and, best of all, Rick in "Casablanca".
Sam	Now I know that one. "Play it again, Sam".
Charlie	That's it.
Sam	*(thinking)* Hey… I've just realised why you keep saying…
Both	Say it again, Sam.
Charlie	Just one of my little Bogie quotes. *(He pours himself a drink of mineral water.)* Although Bogart never did say "Play it

again, Sam".

Sam No?

Charlie One of those Hollywood myths. His co-star, Ingrid Bergman said "Play it, Sam". Bogie said *(With a hint of an American accent.)* "You played it for her. You can play it for me. Play it".

Sam Fancy that. *(She listens off.)* I hear the lift. *(Consults her watch.)* Yes. It's visiting hour. Duty calls. I'll leave you to your book.

Charlie *(toasting her with his plastic cup)* Here's looking at you, kid.

Sam *(with a smile of recognition)* Dirk Bogart!

Charlie Humphrey...

Sam Right. Humphrey Bogarde.

*(As **Sam** goes, she meets **Joanne**. Epitomising the sensible and functional dresser, she eschews any display of bright colour, preferring subdued shades or greys and whites. Heavy glasses, hair shortish or tied back and flat-heeled shoes. An efficient and brisk manner completes the picture. She can be a little younger than **Charlie**.)*

Here she is, Mister Brown. Right on time.

Charlie *(putting his book away in his cabinet)* As always.

Joanne Of course. *(To **Sam**.)* Could you pop these in fresh water for me, Nurse... *(She reads **Sam**'s name badge.)* Samantha Howard? *(She hands **Sam** a very simple bunch of carnations.)*

Sam (taking the flowers) That's me.

Joanne Thank you, Samantha.

Sam I'll see you both later. Bye. *(She exits.)*

Joanne *(going across to **Charlie**)* Hello Charlie. *(She gives him a perfunctory kiss.)*

Charlie Afternoon, Jo. I see you've brought my briefcase. That means business.

Joanne It does indeed. Plenty in the post this morning. *(She pulls some paperwork from the briefcase.)* Another five definite orders.

Charlie Very good.

Joanne Pinnetti have finally renewed their contract.

Charlie Excellent. It took me three trips to secure that one.

Joanne And I've brought your appointment diary right up to date.

Charlie Well done! *(He gives a quick kiss.)* I'm so lucky to have such an efficient wife.

Joanne	Yes, Charlie. I know you didn't marry me for my stunning looks.
Charlie	That's not true, Jo. I couldn't run the business without you.
Joanne	Exactly. *(She gives him a clipboard and pen.)* I need your signature here… and here.
Charlie	(signing) Ah, yes. My order for the new models.
Joanne	Yes. And one other thing. The photocopier is playing up again. Shall I get someone in?
Charlie	Yes, go ahead. Must keep our little office running at full steam. Is that everything?
Joanne	*(putting paperwork back in briefcase)* All done.
Charlie	Great. *(Glances at his watch.)* That leaves us fifty seven minutes.
Joanne	That's nice, Charlie. Still no word about you getting out?
Charlie	Not yet. More tests to be done. You know how it is.
Joanne	At least you're missing all this rotten weather. (She sniffles.) Pass me a tissue will you? *(He gives her the box from the top of his cabinet. She gently blows her nose.)* It's been miserable for days. *(She leaves the tissue box on the bed.)* After you get out, I really wish you'd spend more time at home. At your time of life you should be taking things easier.
Charlie	I'd like to, Jo. But it's cut-throat out there. When I'm not on the road touting for business, my rivals are.
	*(Sam returns. She has **Joanne**'s flowers in a vase.)*
Sam	Excuse me? I'll just pop those here. *(She places the vase on the table.)*
Charlie	Thank you, Nurse Howard.
Sam	No trouble, Mr Brown. *(She picks up the second chair from beside the table.)* And you'll be needing this. *(She places the chair closer to the bed and opposite to where **Joanne** is sitting.)*
Charlie	Another chair? What for?
Sam	For your other visitor.
Charlie	*(for some reason, alarmed)* My other visitor?
Sam	Yes, Mr Brown. Another first for you. You've never had two visitors at the same time before.
Joanne	What a nice surprise for you, Charlie.
Charlie	I don't think so. *(To himself.)* This might be the worst day of my life.
	*(**Evelyn** enters. She is carrying a very decorative bouquet of flowers in gift wrapping. **Evelyn** thinks she's the last word in*

sophisticated elegance; tastefully and expensively dressed with perfectly matched accessories, but it's all a tad too fussy.)

Evelyn	Hello, Charlie.
Charlie	Evie, what are you doing here?
Evelyn	Sorry I missed this morning. Bit of a crisis with the dishwasher. *(She turns to **Sam**.)* If you would be so kind as to arrange these in a suitable vase?
Sam	*(taking the bouquet)* Will do. *(She turns to go.)*
Evelyn	And nurse?
Sam	Yes?
Evelyn	Do remember to cut the stems... horizontally of course. And don't forget to add this. *(She produces a satchel of plant feed from her bag.)*
Sam	Right-oh! *(She exits.)*
Evelyn	Am I not getting a kiss? Anyone would think you weren't pleased to see me. *(He gives her a kiss, only too aware of **Joanne**'s increasingly puzzled expression.)* And why are you wearing those pyjamas and that dreadful dressing gown? Hospital issue, I presume?
Joanne	*(rising)* Certainly not. I brought them.
Evelyn	You? Ah... are you some kind of social worker?
Joanne	Charlie... Aren't you going to introduce me to your lady friend?
Evelyn	His "lady friend"?
Joanne	Charlie?
	(He seems to be paralysed.)
Evelyn	Charlie Brown! Where are your manners? Cat got your tongue? *(But he can't get a word out.)* Really! I'll introduce myself. *(She offers her hand to **Joanne**.)* I'm Mrs Brown. Lovely to meet you.
Joanne	Likewise. I'm Mrs Brown.
Evelyn	Well, well. There's a coincidence. Fancy Charlie's social worker being another Mrs Brown.
Joanne	Excuse me; I am *not* a social worker. Let me explain; I'm Mrs *Charlie* Brown.
Evelyn	That's too much of a coincidence. I am also Mrs *Charlie* Brown.
Joanne	You can't be.
Evelyn	I assure you I am.

Joanne	Charlie! Who is this woman?
Charlie	*(after a big struggle)* She's my wife.
Evelyn	At last. Thank you.
Joanne	But *I'm* your wife.
Evelyn	Has this person escaped from some locked ward?
Joanne	I have not! Charlie - did you, or did you not, marry me seven years ago?
Charlie	Yes Joanne, I did.
Evelyn	That's preposterous! We've been man and wife for twenty one years.
Charlie	We have.
	(The horrible truth begins to sink in.)
Joanne	Are you saying you're married to both of us?
Evelyn	At the same time?
Charlie	Sorry, Evie.
Evelyn	Don't "Evie" me, you lying cheat! *(She advances on him.)*
Charlie	*(retreating)* Now Evie… Evelyn… don't do anything rash.
Evelyn	Rash! I hope for your sake this hospital has an accident and emergency department.
Joanne	*(blocking **Charlie's** retreat)* Every time you said you were "on the road", you were cavorting with her!
Evelyn	Excuse me. I have never "cavorted" in my life. That's what *you* were up to with *my* husband.
Joanne	He's *my* husband too!
Evelyn	Nonsense. You're just his mistress… his fancy woman.
Joanne	I am not a fancy woman!
Evelyn	*(looking her up and down)* That's true. *(She turns on **Charlie**.)* As for you, Charlie Brown! To think I've been married to a bigamist for twenty one years.
Joanne	That's not strictly correct, Evelyn. He only became a bigamist when he married me.
Evelyn	Whose side are you on, Joanne?
Joanne	Not his! There's no possible excuse for his sordid behaviour.
Evelyn	Definitely not! What is your excuse, you… snake in the grass?
Charlie	I haven't any. It just, sort of… happened.
Evelyn	Living with two people at the same time doesn't just "happen". It took big scale planning and deception to keep us apart until now. You must have a second home. So where's your secret love nest?

Joanne	I'd hardly call a small rented flat in the high street a "love nest".
Evelyn	No wonder our paths have never crossed. I'm nearly four miles away at Park Meadows.
Joanne	What? You mean one of those fancy villas with the big gardens?
Evelyn	That's right.
Joanne	Charlie Brown! You've had me cooped up in a poky rented flat while you've spent every penny on her!
Charlie	It's not like that Jo. It's Evie… Evelyn's own place.
Joanne	Don't call me "Jo", you… you… love rat! She's wallowing in luxury compared with me!
Evelyn	I'm not in the habit of wallowing. Even if I did, it's my luxury. I inherited the villa from mother. She was sadly taken before her time while Charlie and I were still engaged. With her last breath, she warned me he was up to no good. Why didn't I listen? Now I know why I see so little of him. He told me he was away on business. Not that I altogether minded. It was a relief not having him around making the place untidy. It also left me free to entertain the bridge club and the floral society and, most importantly, the Women's Guild.
Charlie	I was away on business. Honest.
Joanne	He was. I can vouch for that since I run the business for him.
Evelyn	Yes. I know he has some office somewhere.
Joanne	In the high street, underneath a certain poky rented flat.
Evelyn	I did always imagine some mousy secretary type. *(She looks at Joanne.)* I see I wasn't far out. *(Joanne bristles.)* Charlie Brown, most businessmen hire a secretary. They don't marry one.
Charlie	But Jo… Joanne is so wonderful with the admin. She deserved more.
Evelyn	Why didn't you just give her a pay rise? I presume she goes with you on all your trips to Paris and Milan?
Joanne	To where?
Evelyn	To the fashion houses of Paris and Milan. All my guild ladies are so envious that I'm married to a top designer.
Joanne	A what? Paris and Milan? Charlie's last business trip was to Grimsby.
Evelyn	Grimsby? One doesn't associate Grimsby with haute couture.
Joanne	*(the "mousy secretary" enjoys her revenge)* "One" doesn't.

	"One" associates Grimsby with Charlie's best regular order… for vacuum cleaners.
Evelyn	*(reeling from the worst blow yet)* Vacuum cleaners!
Charlie	Salesman of the year!
Joanne	You were only nominated.
Charlie	It's still a big honour.
Evelyn	I just can't take in what I've found out today. How could you do this to me, Charlie Brown? This is dreadful. When this gets out, I'll never be able to face the Women's Guild again. Not when they hear I've been… *(She is close to tears.)* I've been… married to a vacuum cleaner salesman!
Joanne	At least you see him most of the time. I only see him two days a week.
Evelyn	Only twice a week?
Joanne	Mondays and Wednesdays. Always Mondays and Wednesdays.
Evelyn	Don't complain. I used to see him all the time. Now it's only Tuesdays and Thursdays. And Christmas day… every second year. Now I know why.
Joanne	Same here. Boxing Day last year. Christmas Day the year before.
Charlie	I thought giving you alternate Christmas and Boxing Days was only fair.
Evelyn	Fair!... Fair!!!
Joanne	Wait a minute, Evelyn. Before you commit murder, there's something not adding up here. Charlie, you're with me Mondays and Wednesdays?
Charlie	Without fail.
Joanne	And Evelyn Tuesdays and Thursdays?
Charlie	Always.
Evelyn	We get turn about Christmas and Boxing Day.
Joanne	But I've never, ever, seen you on New Year's Day. Have you, Evelyn?
Evelyn	Not since we were first married.
Joanne	So the question is; what do you get up to at the weekend… not to mention New Year's Day?
	*(As **Charlie** struggles to come up with an answer, **Melissa** makes a big entrance. She is also bearing flowers. Her choice is a large riotously mixed bunch. **Melissa** doesn't know the meaning of the word "subtle". She is wildly flamboyant in dress and attitude, all silky and flowing or*

slinky and revealing - or any combination that makes an impact. Voluptuous red or blonde hair, vivid make-up to match and a husky voice. She doesn't talk about her age.)

Melissa Hi there, lover boy!

Evelyn *(to Joanne)* Happy new year.

Melissa *(blowing him extravagant kisses)* Kiss! Kiss! Kiss!

Charlie Kiss... kiss... *(He starts to return blown kisses but falters under the withering glares of **Joanne** and **Evelyn**.)*

Melissa I know you like me to do evening visiting, but I thought I'd give you a big surprise.

Charlie A surprise? This has to be the worst day of my life.

Melissa Charlie boy, where did you get that dressing gown? They're not transferring you to Colditz?

*(An offended **Joanne** rises.)*

I see you've got visitors. Aren't you going to introduce us?

Joanne Go on Charlie. Do the honours.

*(Further humiliation is temporarily spared by the return of **Sam**.)*

Melissa Hello... Samantha, isn't it?

Sam That's right. *(She takes **Melissa**'s flowers.)* I know. Just pop them in water. Well, isn't this nice, Charlie. All your sisters visiting at the same time. *(Exits.)*

Evelyn His what?

Melissa Your sisters? *(She takes a chair from beside the table.)* Have you been keeping little secrets from me, lover boy?

*(Derisive reactions from **Joanne** and **Evelyn**.)*

Evelyn And who do you imagine you are?

Melissa *(striking a pose)* Me? Why, darling, I'm the one and only Mrs Charlie Brown!

Joanne That's what you think.

Melissa I should know who I am. *(Sits.)* I'm definitely Mrs Brown.

Evelyn *(rising*)* No. *I'm* Mrs Brown. *(*It is essential that the three women leap to their feet in turn with their exclamations of "I'm Mrs Brown" to point the "I'm Spartacus" gag.)*

Joanne *(rising)* I'm Mrs Brown.

Melissa *(rising)* I'm Mrs Brown. *(Thinks.)* Isn't this in a Kirk Douglas film? We can't all be Mrs Brown, can we? I'm Melissa, but you can call me Mel.

Evelyn *(eying **Melissa**'s outfit)* I know what we'd like to call you.

Joanne Now, Evelyn. It's not Melissa's fault. Looks like she's another

	victim like us.
Evelyn	Yes. We've all been had by Mr Deceitful.
Melissa	Charlie, you haven't... with them?
Evelyn	He has. Meet the bigamist of the year.
Melissa	You're having me on. Charlie boy, a bigamist? No. He can't be. We've been man and wife for fourteen years. I've got a marriage certificate to prove it... and I'm wearing his ring. *(**Melissa** flashes her ring. **Joanne** and **Evelyn** respond by displaying their rings. As all three hands are extended for inspection, they all do double takes.)*
Evelyn	Joanne... you've got my ring.
Joanne	Evelyn... your ring is exactly the same as mine... *and* Melissa's.
Melissa	We've all got the same ring!
Evelyn	*(as they all turn to **Charlie**)* Explain, Charlie Brown.
Charlie	It is a nice ring. And the jeweller is an old school chum.
Joanne	So that's why we get a jewellery catalogue in the post every month... and a card every Christmas.
Evelyn	Oh yes, Melissa. He had it all nicely planned. I was his morning visitor. Joanne was afternoon. You were evening.
Charlie	Until that plan went pear-shaped. Of all the hospitals, in all the towns, in all the world, you all walked into mine.
Evelyn	Joanne and I take care of Monday to Thursday. And you?
Melissa	Friday and Saturday.
Evelyn	I run his home. Joanne runs his business. No prizes for guessing your particular role.
Melissa	I'm an independent lady. No man keeps me... or vice versa. I have my own charming pied-á-terre with my specially appointed boudoir.
Joanne	Boudoir? You mean bedroom?
Melissa	No, darling. I mean boudoir. With all kind of extras.
Evelyn	Extras?
Melissa	Little bits and pieces. Just to spice things up, if you get my meaning.
Joanne	We'd rather not.
Melissa	And lover boy never says no.
Evelyn	I don't believe this. Not only a bigamist, but a pervert to boot!
Melissa	Oh, yes! Charlie loves my thigh-length leather...
Evelyn	Are you trying to be deliberately provocative?
Melissa	Darling, I'm always provocative... without trying.

Charlie	I only wanted some excitement.
Joanne	Excitement? The only time I got you excited is when I gave you that letter from the Inland Revenue.
Melissa	Darlings, it's all about making your man happy in bed, without forgetting your own pleasure. Confess, darlings… what makes you happy in bed?
Joanne	Me? An Ovaltine and a good crossword.
Evelyn	I must admit I've never been terribly keen on all that nonsense. How *can* you keep a tidy bedroom?
Melissa	Rumpled sheets… *(Audible intake of breath.)* No wonder Charlie was so eager to sample the pleasures of my boudoir.
Joanne	Charlie, eager? That'll be the day.
Melissa	Believe me, darlings, when I first met lover boy it was lust with a capital "L". Talk about insatiable… But now… *(She sighs.)* The years have taken their toll. Yet there are still nights when I can unleash the wild animal in Charlie.
Evelyn	The only animal I ever see is the one that drops biscuit crumbs on the Axminster.
Melissa	One intriguing question, darlings. What does he call you during those intimate moments?
Evelyn	Those rare moments? He calls me "angel". I used to think it was terribly endearing.
Joanne	He calls me "angel" too, during those very rare moments.
Melissa	"Angel" too… every night. *(She works it out.)* "Charlie's Angels".
Charlie	My little private joke.
Evelyn	Are we laughing?
Charlie	I was worried I'd blurt out the wrong name… you know… in the heat of the passion.
Evelyn	What heat? I'm lucky to get lukewarm. No wonder, Joanne. He was worn out by her. And I always thought it was because of his bad leg.
Melissa	His bad leg?
Joanne	Oh, yes. *(Evelyn nods in agreement.)* Charlie's bad leg does restrict him.
Evelyn	At least we can agree on that.
Joanne	Oh, yes. He did have such a nasty fall.
Evelyn	A fall?
Joanne	Off the south face of the Matterhorn.
Evelyn	He told me it was the piece of shrapnel embedded in his leg

that retired him from the S.A.S.

Charlie   Well... mountaineering was essential training for the S.A... *(He falters under intense glares.)* Sorry, girls. I think I read too many comics as a child.

Evelyn   Serves us right for marrying a man called Charlie Brown.

Melissa   It might have been worse. We might have married a Henry.

Joanne   We might... *(Thinks.)* Why not Henry? *(Thinks more.)* Of course - Henry had six wives.

(The ladies consider this before they are all struck with the same horrifying thought and three heads simultaneously swivel in the direction of the entrance.)

Charlie   I would say, in my defence, I have treated you all equally.

Joanne   No, you haven't. Evelyn and I get alternate nights. Melissa gets you two nights in a row.

Melissa   Believe me, darling. After one night with me, Charlie needs another night to recover.

Evelyn   Charlie Brown... how could you associate with this... floozy... this... strumpet?

Melissa   *(not offended)* I prefer "floozy".

Evelyn   *(getting tearful)* Didn't I give you everything a man could ask for? How many husbands come home to an immaculate house? Not one speck of dust. Everything in its proper place. Cordon bleu meals served on Crown Derby *and* lace napkins.

Charlie   I know, Evelyn. It's just that perfection can sometimes be too perfect.

Evelyn   *(sniffling)* You just don't appreciate me. Twenty one years of betrayal and lying is all I get in return.

*(During this, **Charlie** frantically searches for the box of tissues that was on top of his bedside cabinet. When he can't find it, he quickly grabs another box from inside the cabinet. This box is gaudy with multi-coloured tissues.)*

Charlie   I'm truly sorry, Evie. I didn't mean to hurt anybody.

(He offers her the box. She is about to take a tissue but reacts in horror when she realises what she is being given.)

Evelyn   I didn't give you these!

Charlie   Sorry.

*(He quickly gets another box from his cabinet. This is the expensive looking box in pastel colours. He returns to **Evelyn**, still carrying Melissa's box in his other hand, but makes sure that **Evelyn** is presented with the correct box.)*

Evelyn	*(taking a tissue)* That's better.
Charlie	It's true, Evie. I have a home that any man would envy. But I needed something else.
Evelyn	A good time girl.
Melissa	Guaranteed!
Charlie	But a great home life and a great... other life still wasn't enough.
Joanne	So you married a secretary. *(She is also getting tearful.)* I devoted my life to you.
Charlie	Sorry, Joanne. *(He is about to offer a tissue, but realises that the boxes in each hand belong to **Evelyn** and **Melissa**. He does a quick swap for the plain supermarket box. This is unseen by **Joanne**.)* Here.
Joanne	*(taking a tissue)* I don't know why I'm being emotional. You're not worth it. I really don't know how you got away with it for so long.
Charlie	Who'd ever suspect someone who looks like me? You have to agree, I'm nothing special am I? Rather ordinary, in fact.
Joanne	Very ordinary if truth be told. I can't imagine what I ever saw in you.
Evelyn	Quite. Zero looks and even less charm. Pathetic, really.
Melissa	True. We're not talking God's gift to women, are we?
Charlie	Thanks. You didn't need to agree with me *that* much. It's not easy living a triple life. The worry. The constant fear of slipping up.
Evelyn	But it does help when your hospital has morning, afternoon and evening visiting.
Joanne	I'm the only one who should be here right now.
Evelyn	And to prove that, here's one get well card on display, and it isn't mine. *(She picks it up and reads)* "From your loving wife".
Joanne	That's me. Or that was me.
Evelyn	Where have you hidden my card? *(She approaches his bedside cabinet.)* In here, I presume?
Charlie	*(standing in front of his cabinet.)* You can't go in there. It's private.
Evelyn	*(sharply)* Charlie!
	*(He jumps aside. **Evelyn** begins inspecting the contents. The first item found is his paperback.)*
Evelyn	"Humphrey Bogart". Really.
	(She tosses it aside. The next item discovered is the stylish

get well card that was originally on display.)
Here's my card.
*(She deliberately places it in front of **Joanne**'s card then returns to her search and finds a third get well card. It is a large colourful specimen with a rude and/or tacky design.)*
The least said about this, the better.
(The card is deposited in the bin. A bemused Melissa simply shrugs. The next item produced is a stylish pair of pyjamas.)
Only worn when I'm here presumably?

Charlie   It is a bit stressful changing pyjamas three times a day *and* remembering to wear the right ones.

Joanne   *(sarcastically)* Poor dear.
*(**Evelyn** finds a vividly coloured dressing gown that has the words "Lover Boy" emblazoned on the back in big letters. She holds it with the tips of her fingers as if she was handling something radioactive.)*

Evelyn   Yes… *(To **Melissa**)* How can you cope with life without one iota of taste?
(She casts aside Melissa's choice and returns to her search. The next item found is her bottle of cherry cordial.)
And here's my cherry cordial.
(She picks up Joanne's mineral water.)
Mineral water? How bland.
*(**Joanne**'s mineral water is replaced by **Evelyn**'s choice. The mineral water is also consigned to the bin. Her last discovery is a small can. She holds it up and reads the label.)*
"Red Bull*. For improved performance and increased stamina". *(*or similar popular energy drink)*
(She looks at Charlie. He squirms.)
I wonder who brought this?
*(She diverts her gaze to **Melissa** before the Red Bull also ends up in the bin.)*

Joanne   Look at all the evidence. How did we miss it?

Charlie   I'm just amazed nobody ever suspected.

Evelyn   I did.
*(Joanne and **Melissa** look doubtful.)*
Of course I did. When one starts seeing less and less of one's husband, one does begin to suspect that he's having his bit on the side. But to have *two* bits *and* marry both of them!

Joanne   I object to being called a "bit".

Melissa	And I'd rather be a "floozy".
Joanne	I would point out, Evelyn, that Charlie and I were properly married. *(She swaps the cards on the cabinet so that her card is in front of **Evelyn**'s.)* I have a certificate to prove it. *(She deposits **Evelyn**'s card in the bin.)*
Melissa	And so do I.
Joanne	So don't get superior with us. We're all equal "bits".
Evelyn	Nonsense. Your so-called "marriage certificates" aren't worth the paper they're written on. Besides, I had a formal white wedding in a church. Charlie walked me down the aisle. No doubt you two had grubby ceremonies in some back street registrar's.
Melissa	Au contraire. I insisted on a church wedding... just for a giggle. So I got my walk down the aisle too. How about you, Joanne?
Joanne	I have to admit; Charlie did me proud in church and walked me down the aisle.
Melissa	Charlie, boy, you ought to have blisters.
Evelyn	I fail to see what you find amusing about his reprehensible behaviour. And let's be blunt; neither of your "white" weddings were really "white", were they? And how about guests? We had a full church. Nearly half were Charlie's family and friends. Might one enquire how many of his side turned up for your repeat performances?
Joanne	In my case, none at all.
Evelyn	Just as I thought.
Joanne	They were all travelling down from the north. Charlie told me they got stranded on the motorway in a snow storm. I never questioned it at the time. I should have. We were married in mid-July.
Evelyn	What date in July?
Joanne	The fourteenth.
Evelyn	Was it now? Melissa... when did you and Charlie tie the knot?... Perhaps I should rephrase that.
Melissa	Our happy day was also the fourteenth... of June. And you, Evelyn? Let me take a wild guess at the fourteenth of...
Evelyn	August.
Joanne	Same date, consecutive months. *(They turn to **Charlie** for an explanation.)*
Charlie	It's hard enough remembering one anniversary. You can accuse me of a lot, but I never forgot anybody's anniversary.

Joanne	Why didn't you just choose the first of April?
Evelyn	So, Melissa. Did any of his family make an appearance at your wedding?
Melissa	Not one.
Evelyn	Oh, dear. Another wedding to forget.
Melissa	But a honeymoon to remember.
Evelyn	And what feeble excuse was offered?
Melissa	Our wedding had to be kept quiet because of Charlie's job.
Evelyn	Really? *(Exchanges glance with **Joanne**.)* And what job would that be?
Melissa	Charlie isn't allowed to tell me. *(Confidentially.)* Official Secrets Act.
	*(**Joanne** and **Evelyn** nod in pitying agreement.)*
Evelyn	Yes, Melissa. You never knew? Double-o-seven and a half.
Joanne	Licensed to lie.
Charlie	I only said I worked undercover for MI5.
Evelyn	*(to **Melissa**)* And you believed him?
Joanne	You believed him, Evelyn. *(To **Melissa**)* She thought he was a top fashion designer jetting to Milan and Paris.
Melissa	Even I wouldn't have believed that. I didn't like to spoil his little fantasy.
Evelyn	I was snared by his web of deceit. *(She goes into her handbag.)* Take a look at this. His last postcard from Paris. *(She shows them the offending item.)*
Joanne	That's a French stamp and it's postmarked "Paris".
Melissa	And that's Charlie's writing.
Evelyn	So how on earth?...
	*(They turn to **Charlie** for another explanation.)*
Charlie	Simple, really. Some of the best vacuum cleaners are French and Italian imports. I know this rep who goes regularly. He brings back blank cards, I write them here, and then he takes them back and posts them over there.
Melissa	You have to admire his ingenuity.
Evelyn	I certainly do not! How can you be so flippant about this?
Melissa	You have to laugh.
Joanne	No you don't.
Melissa	I don't know about you two darlings, but it's such a relief not to feel guilty any more.
Charlie	Same here… Wait a minute… Why should you feel guilty? Guilty about what?

Melissa	Charlie, "angel", you don't seriously think you're the only gentleman who samples the pleasures of my boudoir?
Charlie	What? Are you telling me you've been seeing other men? You've been unfaithful?
Joanne	Why are the words "pot", "kettle" and "black" popping into my head right now?
Melissa	I can't help it, lover boy. As you well know, I do have a voracious appetite.
Evelyn	Must you dwell on depravity?
Melissa	Of course Mrs Domestic Goddess would never yield to temptation?
Evelyn	Certainly not. Except…
Charlie	What do you mean "except"? Except what? Except who?
Evelyn	You should know, Charlie. You hired him to come to the house once a week.
Charlie	You mean the gardener? I thought he'd be some old bloke in dungarees.
Evelyn	Oh, no. Young… hunky… in denim.
Charlie	You mean he's been tending to more than the rhododendrons?
Evelyn	*(with a sensual smile)* Mmm…
Melissa	But, Evelyn… those muddy boots on the carpet?
Evelyn	I never allow him anywhere inside the house.
Charlie	Where then?
Evelyn	The potting shed.
Charlie	So you've been… And Mel's been… What next?
	*(**Joanne** becomes aware that all eyes are now on her.)*
Joanne	Me? Don't be ridiculous. *(But they are all still looking at her.)* Well… All right…But only the one time.
Melissa	Reveal all, darling. We did.
Joanne	Remember Charlie, last winter… I had to get someone in to fix the washing machine?
Charlie	A plumber!
Joanne	He *was* fully qualified.
Charlie	You can forget about getting anybody for the photocopier!
Evelyn	Don't you dare look outraged, Charlie Brown. It's all your fault.
Joanne	Yes. You've only yourself to blame. If you'd been around most of the time, like a proper husband.
Evelyn	You wouldn't need a gardener.

Joanne	The washing machine was only a loose pipe you could have fixed.
Melissa	Most men are content with an affair, but you had to marry all three of us.
Charlie	I didn't want to let anybody down. I've always had this problem that I can never say no.
Joanne	Our problem was saying yes.
Charlie	The three of you give me everything I could ask for.
Joanne	But not at the same time.
Evelyn	You might be satisfied. But what about us?
Joanne	Yes. What about our satisfaction?
Melissa	Charlie's never disappointed me yet.
Joanne	I was referring to simple needs like holidays.
Charlie	I take you on holiday.
Joanne	Every three years!
Charlie	But I'm taking you to Gran Canaria next year. It's Evie's turn this year.
Joanne	No, Charlie. I refuse to be a third any more.
Evelyn	I agree. We've heard enough from this three-timer. *(She produces a mobile phone.)* Ladies, it's time for action.
Charlie	What are you going to do?
Evelyn	I propose to begin with the Police. Bigamy is a crime and I want my day in court. After that, we start divorce proceedings.
Charlie	You all want divorces?
Joanne	One divorce and two annulments to be precise. We can argue later over which of us gets the divorce.
Charlie	Three legal cases?
Melissa	Look on the bright side, Charlie. You'll start getting another regular Christmas card… from your lawyer.
Evelyn	*(mobile ready)* I take it we're all agreed?
Melissa	Hold on, girls. Let's think about this. What happens if we involve the Police?
Evelyn	We get justice.
Melissa	Certainly. And just as certainly we'll get lots of publicity.
Joanne	Oh, no!
Melissa	Oh, yes. Picture the tabloid headlines when this gets out. Picture a media frenzy outside your front door.
Evelyn	My god! What would my neighbours say?
Charlie	You're worried about the neighbours?

Evelyn	It's fine for you just dropping in twice a week. I have to live with our neighbours all the time. Imagine the scandal!
Melissa	I love scandal.
Joanne	You would!
Evelyn	I'd have to resign from the Guild committee.
Joanne	But surely the press would treat us sympathetically?
Melissa	You think? We'd be the silly gullible women who got duped. He'd be a matrimonial Robin Hood.
Charlie	Yes! I'd never need to sell another vacuum cleaner. I can see it now... "My Triple Sex Life". A "Sun" exclusive. Interviews. The best-selling book. TV celebrity slots. Hollywood! "Russell Crowe* is Charlie Brown". *(*Or substitute another Hollywood leading man.)*
Evelyn	Oh, no, you won't!
Joanne	Not if Mel is suggesting what I think she's suggesting; that nothing goes beyond this room.
Melissa	It's our decision.
Charlie	Don't I have a say in this?
All Three Wives	No!
Charlie	Couldn't we simply... carry on as we are?
All Three Wives	No!
Evelyn	Especially the "carrying on" bit.
Joanne	Yes. After today, there can only be one Mrs Brown.
Evelyn	You're right. The question is; which one of us?
Melissa	So who's it going to be, lover boy? Come to my boudoir and relish seven nights of unbridled passion. *(Charlie visibly quails at the prospect.)* I'm sure my other gentlemen would understand.
Evelyn	I'm not letting you anywhere near her den of iniquity. Come to Park Meadows and savour seven days of domestic bliss. I can put off the Women's Guild.
Joanne	Wouldn't you rather relax at our comfy little flat? I could tuck you in bed with a hot Ovaltine. You'd get a decent night's sleep and you can drop as many biscuit crumbs as you like.
Evelyn	I married him first. That makes me legally number one.
Joanne	He's due me at least another seven years.
Melissa	Let's draw straws or put our names in a hat... or we let Charlie decide.
Joanne	Yes. You make the choice, Charlie.
Evelyn	Well, Charlie?

Melissa   Decision time, lover boy.

*(A long pause. **Charlie** is looking terribly serious.)*

Charlie   All right. *(He steels himself.)* I'm actually glad you're all here together. It makes it easier to tell you.

Joanne   To tell us what?

Charlie   You know I've been getting lots of tests?

Evelyn   Yes.

Charlie   Well… *(Deep breath.)* The consultant came to see me this morning about the results.

Evelyn   What did he say? *(Pause.)* Charlie... what are you holding back?

Charlie   You'll all need to be very brave.

Melissa   It's not serious…

Charlie   *(gravely)* Very. The worst possible diagnosis. I'm incurable. There's nothing they can do for me.

Joanne   How long have you got?

Evelyn   Months?

Charlie   Days. It's too far advanced. That's the hard truth girls. Cross my heart and hope to… *(He chokes on the last word.)*

Melissa   So you won't be coming home to any of us?

Charlie   I'm afraid not.

Evelyn   There must be something we can do?

Charlie   There is. Let's spare ourselves long goodbyes. I want you all to leave here today and never see me again.

Joanne   No, Charlie. We can't do that.

Charlie   You must. You've got to walk out of this room and get into that lift. If you don't, you'll regret it. Maybe not today, maybe not tomorrow, but soon, and for the rest of your life.

*(As **Charlie** gets into his stride, that hint of an American accent creeps in.)*

Look, girls, I'm not good at being noble. But it doesn't take much to see that the problems of four little people don't amount to a hill of beans in this crazy world.

Evelyn   But we're still your wives.

Charlie   You must remember this; a ring is just a ring, a marriage certificate is just a… piece of paper. You can all make a fresh start. Just go. You'll forget all about me… as time goes by.

*(This has left the three ladies very emotional. **Charlie** quickly hands out boxes of tissues. Needless to say, everybody*

*ends up with the wrong box, but they absently sort it out amongst themselves. The ladies sniffle while **Charlie** looks suitably doomed. Three tissues are drawn simultaneously and they let out a wail that wouldn't shame the chorus in a Greek tragedy. This is the cue for **Sam**, who bounces in, all bright and breezy.)*

Sam	Hello, everybody! Just thought I'd let you know; about ten minutes left. My, we're all looking a bit serious.
Joanne	Yes. Charlie's just told us his news.
Evelyn	From the consultant.
Sam	*(solemnly)* Yes. *(Then her usual self.)* Wasn't it wonderful?
Melissa	Wonderful!
Sam	Yes. Charlie getting the all-clear. Turns out he's in the best of health.
Evelyn	Is he now?
	(Three tissues drop simultaneously to the floor.)
Sam	Isn't it great? It's also the all-clear for Charlie and me.
Joanne	For Charlie and you?
Sam	Charlie! You promised me you'd tell your sisters. He's made me the happiest girl in the world. I'm going to be Mrs Charlie Brown! I know I won't see him very often. I'm happy to accept that as the wife of an international diamond trader. But as Charlie put it; we'll always have Sundays.
	*(There is an ominous silence. **Charlie** just wants the ground to swallow him up. Only **Sam**, in her own happy little world, is unaware of this.)*
Joanne	Ladies… shall we show Samantha something?
	(All three wives display their respective rings.)
Sam	You're all married. That's nice. *(Then she realises.)* Hang on! You've all got the same ring!
	(She reaches into the pocket of her uniform and brings out a ring box. She opens it and compares her ring with the others. The horrible truth strikes her immediately.)
Sam	Charlie Brown! You!...
	(She throws the ring box at him and storms out.)
Charlie	No question. This is definitely the worst day of my life.
Evelyn	So, you think you've had the all-clear? *(She throws aside her box of tissues.)*
Melissa	Think you're in the best of health? *(Ditto.)*
Joanne	Think again. *(Ditto.)*
	(As he retreats to his bed, the ladies create a chilling

impression of circling sharks.)

Melissa   The worst day of your life, lover boy?

Evelyn   Oh, no…

Joanne   It's only just beginning.

*(As they close in, **Sam** returns. As she steps forward, the lighting suddenly dims and she is bathed in an eerie green light like something out of a horror film, loudly accompanied by the shrill stabbing violin glissandos from Bernard Hermann's score for the shower room murder in Alfred Hitchcock's "Psycho". **Sam** has an uncharacteristically nasty look on her face. But that's not half as nasty as what she is brandishing in her hand - a giant hypodermic that a prehistoric vet might have used to sedate a T-Rex. **Charlie** reacts in terror as **Sam** tries a test squirt. The music ends abruptly and the lighting returns to normal, but **Charlie**'s nightmare is far from over.)*

Sam   *(hypodermic ready)* Allow me, "sisters"?

*(**Charlie** cowers on his bed as he is surrounded. Just when **Sam** is poised to strike, there is a snap blackout. In the darkness, we hear a painful howl.)*

Curtain

Furniture & Property List
On Stage

On top of locker:	Plastic cup.
	Tasteful and expensive "get well" card.
	Bottle of cherry cordial.
Inside locker:	Plain "get well" card.
	Garish, tacky and/or rude "get well" card.
	Bottle of mineral water.
	Can of "Red Bull". *(or similar energy drink)*
	Stylish and tasteful pyjamas.
	Loudly coloured dressing gown.
	Box of plain supermarket tissues.
	Gaudy box of coloured tissues.
On top of table:	Magazines.
	Newspapers.
	One or two paperback books.
Off Stage:	Vase for flowers *(Samantha)*
	Large hypodermic *(Samantha)*

Personal

Charlie	Paperback. *(Biography of Humphrey Bogart)*
	Wristwatch.
	Patient identity wristband.
Samantha	Nurse's watch.
	Identity/Security badge
	Jeweller's box containing wedding ring.
Joanne	Simple bunch of plainly wrapped flowers.
	Briefcase containing paperwork, pen and clipboard.
	Wedding ring.*
Evelyn	Expensive bouquet of flowers in gift wrapping.
	Handbag containing plant feed, postcard and mobile phone. Wedding ring.*
Melissa	Extravagantly wild and colourful bunch of flowers.
	Wedding Ring.*
	*Identical *(or as identical as possible from a distance)*
(Please note	*Props are vitally important in this play as their appearance clearly and contrastingly reflect the personalities of the characters who present them. The accurate placement of those props is equally important.)*

Sound Effects

To Open:	"As Time Goes By" from the film "Casablanca"
Page 27:	The shower room murder music from Alfred Hitchcock's film "Psycho".

Lighting

Practical fittings required none

To Open:	General interior lighting.
Cue 1 (Page 27)	
Joanne	"It's only just beginning." Dim general lighting and cross fade to green spot on Sam. *(cue in conjunction with "Psycho" music)*
Cue 2 (Page 27)	Revert to general lighting.
Cue 3 (Page 27)	
Sam	"Allow me, 'sisters'?" Snap black out.